Remember the children
we once were.
The children who wondered
and asked,
wished and hoped,
without thinking of
every consequence.

From the heart,
with the refreshment
and curiosity of life's beginnings,
the most innocent of emotions.

Remember the bravery.
We owned our world.

Keep the light shining! Geynne'Lou Allen

The Hope Star

Best wishes,
Joyce L. Cordee
December, 2001

Collector's Edition
Copyright © 1999 by Jayne A. Cordes
All rights reserved.
Published by J. Kid Productions, Ltd.

First edition, 1999
Designed by
Chris Thomas for David Uhl Studios
Edited by Loretta Hudson

Library of Congress Card Number: 0-097-95119
Cordes, Jayne A.
The Hope Star / Jayne A. Cordes;
illustrated by Gwynne Lee Allen.
ISBN 0-9662670-0-1

Special thanks to:
Michael and Nancy Fox, Susan and Steve Hritz, David Acker,
Chris Thomas, David Gertz and everyone else who believes,
you know who you are.

J. Kid Productions, Ltd.™

The Hope Star

Written by
Jayne A Cordes

Artistry by
Gwynne Lee Allen

From your Mama to B. Hanning and Harry.
From your daughter to Mom and Dad.
From your sister to Debbie, Gwynne, Wendy, Linda,
Susan, Nancy and Frannie.
To Greg who inspired my original story.
And to all the children and adults of the world, may
everything you hope for be seen as a special sparkle
in your eyes, every day, for as long as time.

Many questions are asked on nights
of bright stars and quiet
talking winds...

The night whispers, can you hear it my children?
Your Mama is here and listening with you.
We can talk to a star in the night sky.
The star is called Hope.

See the Hope Star, there in the sky?
See it in its brilliance?
The Hope Star shines like a million diamonds.

Mama, what is the Hope Star?

The Hope Star appears to remind us
of how wonderful it is to believe.
The Hope Star loves to hear your hopes and dreams.

What do we say to the Hope Star?
You whisper your hopes.
What is hope, Mama?
Hope means to believe a wish, a miracle,
a dream, a prayer, a gift or anything your
heart desires, will happen.

The Hope Star has been in the sky for a very, very long time. Its light brilliantly shines on as we whisper loving thoughts for each other and our world.

Children, there is always hope in life.
Even when the Hope Star is hidden by
clouds that wander about, it is still there.
It shines unnoticed, in a magnificent, sunny sky.

The Hope Star's bright light will always
stay in a good and loving heart.

Mama, what have you wished for?
I remember, as a little girl, sitting in a magical place.
I thought of love and happiness in my world and the
hope that I would have children, just like you.

The world we live in is a gift from hope,
the hope born from love, like you and the baby.
What came to me, I wished for.

Children, the Hope Star is here. As you whisper, see all
the bright stars in the sky that sparkle so special for you.
These are your wishes, waiting to happen.

Believe in hope and your dreams will come true,
like they did for me,
when I dreamt of you.

You are here.
My hopes.
My dreams.
My children.

World Hope Products™ introduces *The Hope Star,* the first in a series of engaging story books and collectibles. *The Hope Star's* message - "there is always hope in life", spans generations. This fundamental topic is portrayed in the heartwarming story line of a mother inspiring hope in her young children.

World Hope Products™ was created as an educational umbrella to present valuable concepts to enrich children's lives.

World Hope Products™ is a benefactor to Nonprofit Organizations. A percentage of sales proceeds from World Hope Products™ are designated to World Hope Charities℠ which assigns funds to world charities.

Published by J. Kid Productions, Ltd., Denver, Colorado
Toll free 888.858.5543.
Within the Denver area 303.850.7740.
Visit our website at THEHOPESTAR.COM